LEARN TO READ

JONATHAN JAMES

"Let's Play Ball"

by Crystal Bowman
illustrated by Karen Maizel

ZondervanPublishingHouse
Grand Rapids, Michigan

A Division of HarperCollins*Publishers*

Jonathan James Says, "Let's Play Ball"
Copyright © 1995 by Crystal Bowman
Illustrations copyright © 1995 by Karen Maizel

Requests for information should be addressed to:
Zondervan Publishing House
Grand Rapids, Michigan 49530

Library of Congress Cataloging-in-Publication Data

Bowman, Crystal.
    Jonathan James says, "Let's play ball" / by Crystal Bowman.
       p. cm. — (Jonathan James)
    Summary: Jonathan the rabbit learns from his mother that God made
him to be good at something, and from his father that he must care for his
body, while from Grandma he learns to bat the ball.
    ISBN: 0-310-49621-7
    [1. Rabbits—Fiction.   2. Baseball—Fiction.   3. Grandmothers—Fiction.
3. Christian Life—Fiction.]   I. Title. II. Series: Bowman, Crystal.
Jonathan James.
PZ7.B6834Jv 1995
[E]—dc20   95-6661
                                                  CIP
                                                  AC

Edited by Lori J. Walburg and Leslie Kimmelman
Cover design by Steven M. Scott
Art direction by Chris Gannon
Illustrations and interior design by Karen Maizel

96 97 98 99 /❖ DP / 10 9 8 7 6 5 4 3

To my daughter, Teri,
who likes ice cream for breakfast

With special thanks
to Lori, Leslie, and Jack
—C. B.

For Jenn,
my comfortable pajamas
—K. M.

CONTENTS

JONATHAN STRIKES OUT

It was Saturday.

Jonathan James went out to play.

He swung back and forth in his swing.

He went up and down the slide.

Then he played in his sandbox.

Jonathan saw his friend Jason

coming toward him.

"Hi, J.J.," said Jason.

"Do you want to play?"

"Sure," said Jonathan.

"We can swing and slide.

We can play in my sandbox."

"I do not want to swing and slide,"
said Jason.

"I do not want to play
in your sandbox.

I want to play baseball."

"Okay," said Jonathan,

"let's play baseball."

Jonathan got his ball and bat.

"I will hit first," said Jason.

"Throw the ball to me."

Jonathan threw the ball to Jason.

Jason hit the ball hard.

Jonathan ran after the ball.

"That's one for me!" shouted Jason.

"Pitch me another one!"

Jonathan threw the ball to Jason.

Again Jason hit the ball hard.

Jonathan ran after the ball.

"That's two for me!" shouted Jason.

"Pitch me another one!"

Again and again

Jason hit the ball.

Again and again

Jonathan ran after the ball.

"This is no fun," Jonathan declared.

"I want a turn at bat."

"All right," said Jason.

Jonathan and Jason switched places.

Jason threw the ball to Jonathan.

Jonathan swung the bat.

But he did not hit the ball.

"Strike one!" shouted Jason.

"Try again."

Jason threw the ball.

Jonathan swung the bat.

But he missed once more.

Again and again

Jason threw the ball to Jonathan.

Again and again

Jonathan swung the bat.

But he could not hit the ball.

"I give up!" said Jonathan.

"I guess I'm just no good at baseball."

"I guess not," said Jason.

"I am finished playing anyway.

I'm going home."

"Good-bye," said Jonathan sadly.

Just then Mother came outside
with Jonathan's little sister, Kelly.
"Hi there, J.J." said Mother.
"Why are you so sad?"
"I am no good at baseball,"
said Jonathan.
"I cannot hit the ball.
Jason hits the ball every time."
"Well," said Mother,

"Jason may be good at baseball,
but you are good at other things.
You can run fast and climb high.
You are good at drawing pictures,
and you are good at
being a big brother.
Some people are good at some things,
and other people are good
at other things.
That is the way God made us."

"But I want to be good at baseball,"
said Jonathan.

"Well," Mother told him,
"if you practice hard,
you might be good at baseball, too."

"Really?" Jonathan asked.

"Really!" Mother said.

Jonathan pushed Kelly in the swing.

They went up and down the slide.

Then they played in the sandbox.

It was a lot of fun.

"Maybe I will practice
baseball tomorrow,"
Jonathan told Mother.

"But today I will practice
being a good big brother."

Mother smiled.

"Good idea," she said.

ICE CREAM FOR BREAKFAST

It was morning.

Jonathan was hungry.

He put two scoops

of ice cream in a bowl.

Then he poured chocolate syrup

over the ice cream.

Father came into the kitchen.

"What are you doing, J.J.?"
asked Father.

"Eating ice cream," Jonathan said.

"But it is time for breakfast,"
said Father.

"Ice cream is not breakfast food."

"What does it matter?"
asked Jonathan.

"I like ice cream."

"I know you like ice cream,"
Father told him.

"Ice cream is okay
for a snack or dessert.
But you must eat
good food for breakfast."

"Why?" asked Jonathan.

"Because you are a growing boy,"
Father explained.
"If you do not eat good food,
you will not be big and strong.
You will not be able to run and jump.
You will not be able to play baseball."
Jonathan wanted to be big and strong.
He wanted to run and jump.
And he wanted to play baseball.

"Besides," Father added,

"God wants us

to take care of our bodies."

"How do we do that?" asked

Jonathan.

"Well," said Father,

"we take care of our bodies

when we exercise and rest.

And we take care of our bodies

when we eat food that is good for us."

"May I save my ice cream for later?"

asked Jonathan.

"Yes." Father nodded.

"You may put it in the freezer."

"Well then," said Jonathan,

"what's for breakfast?"

"I will make you
a baseball player's breakfast,"
said Father.

"Okay!" said Jonathan.

Jonathan waited
while Father made his breakfast.

"Here it is!" said Father.

Father brought Jonathan
a banana, a bowl of oatmeal,
and a big glass of orange juice.

Just then Mother came
into the kitchen.

"What a good breakfast," said Mother.

"May I have some?"

"No," said Jonathan.

"This is a baseball player's breakfast.

You are not a baseball player.

But you may have my ice cream.

It is in the freezer."

Mother and Father laughed.

And Jonathan ate his breakfast.

GRANDMA PLAYS BALL

"Will you teach me
how to play baseball?"
Jonathan asked Father.
"Oh," said Father,
"I would like to play baseball,
but today I have to go to work.
We can play when I get home."
Jonathan sighed.
He did not want to wait
until Father got home.
He wanted to play baseball now.

"Will you teach me
how to play baseball?"
Jonathan asked Mother.
"I am sorry," said Mother.
"I cannot play with you now.
Why don't you play baseball
with Kelly?"
"She is too little," Jonathan said.
"She cannot teach me
how to play baseball.
I guess I will never learn."

Jonathan went to his bedroom.

He looked out his window.

It was sunny and warm,

a perfect day for baseball.

But there was no one to play with.

Then Jonathan saw someone
riding a bicycle.
It was Grandma!
Jonathan ran outside to meet her.
"Hi, Grandma," said Jonathan.
"Hi, there, J.J.," said Grandma.
"What are you doing today?"
"Nothing," said Jonathan.
"I want to play baseball,
but there is no one to play with."

"Well," said Grandma,
"I will play baseball with you."
"I am not very good," said Jonathan.
"That's okay," said Grandma.
"Maybe you just need to practice."
Grandma and Jonathan
went into the backyard.
Jonathan got his ball and bat.
Grandma threw the ball to Jonathan.
Jonathan swung at the ball,
but he did not hit it.
"See," said Jonathan.
"I told you I was no good."

"You need another bat,"

said Grandma.

Grandma looked in the garage.

She found a big, red bat.

"This one is much better," she said.

Grandma threw the ball to Jonathan.

Jonathan swung at the ball,

but he did not hit it.

"Good try," said Grandma.

"But something is missing.

Do you have a baseball cap?"

"Yes," said Jonathan.

"Well, go and get it," said Grandma.

"If you want to be a baseball player,

you need to look like one."

Jonathan got his baseball cap

and put it on.

Grandma threw the ball to Jonathan.

Jonathan swung at the ball.

He was close, but he did not hit it.

"Almost!" Grandma called.

"I think you need some gum.

Baseball players chew gum.

I have some in my pocket."

Grandma gave Jonathan

a piece of gum.

It tasted good.

"Now you are ready to play,"
said Grandma.
"You have the right bat.
You have your baseball cap on.
And you have some gum.
Now you can hit the ball."
Grandma threw the ball to Jonathan.
Jonathan swung at the ball,
and this time he hit it!

"Good hit!" shouted Grandma.

"I knew you could do it.

You just needed the right stuff."

"And someone to teach me,"

said Jonathan.

Jonathan was so happy!

Grandma and Jonathan
played baseball all afternoon.
Mother and Father asked Grandma
to stay for supper.
At the dinner table,
Jonathan thanked God for Grandma,
and Grandma thanked God
for Jonathan.
After dinner, they all went outside
to play baseball.

And Jonathan hit the ball every time.

A VISIT TO THE HOSPITAL

Mother was talking on the telephone.

Jonathan could tell

something was wrong.

Mother looked very worried.

Jonathan began to worry too.

Jonathan waited while Mother talked.

Finally she hung up the phone.

"What is wrong?" asked Jonathan.

"Grandma is in the hospital,"
said Mother.

"Why?" asked Jonathan. "Is she sick?"

"No," said Mother. "She is not sick.

Grandma is hurt.

She fell off her bicycle."

Jonathan started to cry.

"Is she going to be all right?"
he asked.

"Oh, yes," said Mother.

"Grandma will be fine.

She just broke her arm."

Jonathan was glad that Grandma
would be all right.
But he was still worried.
He thought about her
lying in the hospital.
He thought about her broken arm.
Jonathan wondered
if Grandma was sad.
He wondered if she was scared.

"We can visit Grandma
this afternoon," said Mother.
"Oh, good!" said Jonathan.
"Can we bring her something?"
"Well," said Mother,
"we could pick some flowers
and put them in a vase."
"Yes," said Jonathan.
"And I could make her a picture."
"Oh, yes," said Mother.
"Grandma would like that."

Jonathan, Kelly, and Mother
went outside to pick flowers.
Mother put them in a pretty vase.
Then Jonathan made Grandma
a picture.
Kelly made a picture, too.
Jonathan drew a picture
of Grandma and him playing
baseball.
Then he colored it.

He drew a happy sun in the sky,
and he wrote GET WELL SOON
at the top.
"Grandma will like this,"
said Jonathan.
Kelly's picture was a mess.
All she did was scribble.
But Jonathan knew that Grandma
would like her picture, too.

Before they went to the hospital
Jonathan prayed.
He asked God to be with Grandma
and to make her better.

When they got to the hospital,
Jonathan was surprised.
Grandma was smiling and talking.

She did not look sad.

She did not look scared.

"Well, hello there!" said Grandma.

"I am happy you came to see me."

Mother gave Grandma the flowers.

Jonathan and Kelly gave her

their pictures.

"Why, thank you," said Grandma.

"These are beautiful."

"You're welcome," said Jonathan.

"I like your picture, J. J.,"
said Grandma.

"We had fun playing baseball,
didn't we?"

"Do you like my picture?" asked Kelly.

"Oh, yes," said Grandma.

"It is a very pretty design."

Jonathan sat in a chair
next to Grandma's bed.

"Can we watch TV?" asked Jonathan.

"Sure," Grandma agreed.

She turned on the TV.

"Oh, look!" said Jonathan.

"A baseball game!"

Jonathan had fun watching
the baseball game with Grandma.

Then it was time to go.

"I'll see you tomorrow,"

said Grandma.

Jonathan was surprised.

"Are we coming to the hospital

again tomorrow?" he asked.

"Oh, no," said Mother.

"Grandma is coming to our house.

She is going to stay with us

until her arm gets better."

"Oh, good!" said Jonathan.

"It will be fun having

Grandma at our house.

We can read books and play games."

"And when my arm gets better,"

said Grandma, "we can play baseball."

Jonathan smiled.

He was glad that Grandma

was going to be all right.

GET WELL SOON

READ UP ON THE ADVENTURES OF JONATHAN JAMES!

Jonathan James Says, "I Can Be Brave"

Book 1   ISBN 0-310-49591-1

Jonathan James is afraid. His new bedroom is too dark. He's going into first grade. And he has to stay at Grandma's overnight for the first time. What should he do? These four lively, humorous stories will show new readers that sometimes things that seemed scary can actually be fun.

Jonathan James Says, "Let's Be Friends"

Book 2   ISBN 0-310-49601-2

Jonathan James is making new friends! In four easy-to-read stories, Jonathan meets a missionary, a physically challenged boy, and a new neighbor. New readers will learn important lessons about friendship. And they will learn that our friends like us just for being who we are.

Jonathan James Says, "I Can Help"

Book 3   ISBN 0-310-49611-X

Jonathan James is growing up–and that means he can help! In four chapters written especially for new readers, Jonathan James learns to pitch in and help his family–sometimes successfully, sometimes not. Young readers will learn that they, too, have ways they can help.

Jonathan James Says, "Let's Play Ball"

Book 4   ISBN 0-310-49621-7

Jonathan James wants to learn how to play baseball. Who will teach him? Will he ever hit the ball? Four fun-filled chapters show young readers that, with practice, they too can succeed in whatever they try.

Look for all the books in the Jonathan James series at your local Christian bookstore.

📖 ZondervanPublishingHouse
5300 Patterson S.E. • Grand Rapids, MI 49530

Crystal Bowman lives with her family in Grand Rapids, Michigan. A former schoolteacher, she enjoys writing for children. "I hope that my stories help boys and girls understand more about God," she says. Besides writing, Crystal enjoys watching her boys play tennis and hockey, and she goes to all her daughter's softball games.

Karen Maizel is a graduate of the Art Institute of Pittsburgh and started her career as a fashion illustrator. "I always wanted to illustrate books for children," she says. "So when I was raising my daughters, I took children's books out of the library and studied the pictures. Then I trained myself and kept drawing to improve the quality of my art." Karen's hard work paid off with the Jonathan James series, her first book project for children.

Crystal and Karen would love to hear from you. You may write them at:

Author Relations
Zondervan Publishing House
5300 Patterson Ave., S.E.
Grand Rapids, MI 49530